This book belongs to

_____

The Steadfast Tin Soldier

ILLUSTRATED BY

David Delamare

AS TOLD BY

Katie Campbell

FROM A STORY BY

Hans Christian Andersen

BARNES
&NOBLE
BOOKS
NEW YORK

There was once a troop of gallant tin soldiers, twenty-five to be exact, all brothers, as they had all been made from the same tin spoon. Each little man rested his gun firmly against his shoulder, always standing straight and proud, and, of course, keeping his eyes well to the front. They all wore the most splendid uniform of red and blue, with high-top cap, snug white gloves, and shiny black boots. For a long time they waited in readiness within the dark recesses of their tin lodging. Finally the day arrived when the lid was lifted, and the smiling face of a little boy peered down into the box. Clapping his hands with delight, he cried out, "Oh, look! Soldiers, tin soldiers!"

It was the little boy's birthday and the tin soldiers were his grandest present, so he wasted no time in setting them up. All of the soldiers were just exactly alike, with the exception of one, who differed from the rest in having only one leg. You see, he had been the last to be made, and before he could be finished the tin had simply run out. But, nonetheless, he stood just as proudly and firmly on his one leg as the others did on two. In fact, this story is about this very same soldier's brave adventures.

The little boy had played with the soldiers all afternoon, drilling the troops and arranging them in formation in preparation to do battle—if need be. It felt good to be needed, and the tin soldier took pride in the fact that he performed his duties so honorably.

When the boy had finished instructing the troops, they were left on the table alongside many other wonderful toys. As the tin soldier began to look at the new world before him, he caught sight of an elegant paper castle. This was something special indeed, for he could see right through the tiny windows into the finely furnished rooms. And there were little trees too, surrounding a small mirror, which served as a lake on which porcelain swans gently glided.

But the most wonderful thing of all, without question, was the pretty maiden that stood just outside the door to the castle. She was made of paper too, yes, but she wore a dress of the very finest silk, dyed pink, with a tiny white-laced doily draped gracefully about her shoulders and pinned with a beautiful spangle. She was in a charming pose, both arms extended, one raised slightly higher than the other, with a gentle tilt like the stately dip of a swan's neck. For you see, she was a dancer. And in her dance she raised one of her legs so high that the tin solider could see nothing of it, and he thought that she too must have but one leg.

If tin soldiers could blush, he certainly would have, for never had he seen such beauty as the maiden that danced before him. "She would make a most excellent wife!" he thought; "But I am but a lowly soldier, living in a box, and with my twenty-four brothers at that! And look at her, living in that splendid palace and being so . . . so very beautiful! But still, there would be no harm in just trying to meet her."

When he was sure no one was around he moved over to a silver snuffbox and lay down behind it. From there, unseen, he could watch the little dancer for hours. As night fell the other soldiers were put away in their box, and the family went off to bed.

Under the cover of night—the magic time— stirred to life the little boy's playthings. For night was the time when the toys would play. And play they did. They gave grand balls and passed many pleasant hours visiting one another. The hobby horses held races and the kites flew over the dance floor as nutcrackers bowed and asked the favor of a waltz from the pretty porcelain dolls. The tin soldiers rustled about and banged on their box, for they wished to join the fun, but unhappily they found they were unable to lift the lid. The pet canary joined in too, and recited sweet verse to the chess set, as the kings and queens were closely attended by their courts. But the tin soldier and the dancer never moved once, she content to stand poised on one tiptoe, and he to gaze upon her beauty.

As the moon shone full through the window, and the clock struck midnight, up came the lid of the snuff-box with a bang! But what rose out of the box was not a whirl of snuff. Oh, no! There came a-creeping a wicked black goblin, full of mischief in his little cold heart. The toys fell back and shook with fright, for they knew what an evil devil he could be. But not the tin soldier; he stood brave and pretended to ignore the goblin's vile curses.

The goblin spoke in a shrill voice:

"Tin soldier! Be mindful of your ways,
And no more attention will you pay,
To the little maiden who dances so sweet.

"For if you persist to try and meet,
You'll find yourself trod under these feet,
And crushed like a harvest of fine winter wheat.

"So, forego all thoughts of your tin heart,
And return at once to the soldiers' box,
Or wicked curse and charm I'll work,
Upon your soul I'll now impart!"

So saying, the goblin waited for a reply, but the tin soldier held firm and said nothing. The goblin was furious. He puffed up his slimy frame and spit full, the loathsome wretch, then said:

"Ah! you just wait until tomorrow,
For misery on the wing is sure to follow!"

The goblin then slid back into the snuffbox, grabbing the lid and slamming it shut.

When morning arrived the children got up to play and immediately placed the tin soldier on the windowsill. Now whether by goblin mischief or simply a gust of wind, it cannot be said, but the window flew open and the brave little soldier tumbled headlong down to the street. It was a terrific fall, but luckily, his bayonet stuck in a crack in the pavement, saving him from landing on his head. And though the children looked everywhere for him, nearly stepping on him at times, they were unable to see him. If only he had cried out, "Look here, over here I am!" then they would surely have found him. But being the proud soldier that indeed he was, he did not think it proper to be going about shouting this and that while in full uniform.

Before long the sky grew dark and heavy. Gusts of wind kicked up dust and whirled it into the poor soldier's eyes. Then came a furious storm with pounding rain and clapping thunder. The brave soldier held fast, though doubtless he was a bit unnerved. When the storm had passed, two young boys came along and one spied the unhappy toy.

"Look there!" said one. "A tin soldier. Let's take him for a boatride."

They took an old newspaper and folded it into the shape of a little boat; then, placing the tin soldier in the middle, they let it loose to sail down the gutter. The boys ran alongside, cheering and clapping as the boat went faster and faster. Oh, my goodness! The waves were thrashing the boat right and left, and tossing it to and fro. Up and down, up and down the boat would go on top of the waves. Then round and round, round and round as it whirled about in the current. The poor tin soldier was becoming quite dizzy and hoped he would not become seasick. Suddenly the soldier found himself surrounded in darkness as the boat flew down into a street drain.

"Oh, curse that goblin! Just look at the mess he has gotten me into!" he said to himself. "Now where am I? If I only had the little dancer to share this ride with me, then I wouldn't care how dark it is or where I am going."

At that very moment a giant water rat—and a very grumpy one at that, having lived all his life in this dark tunnel—came waddling alongside the little boat.

"Show us your pass, yesss . . . yesss . . . show us your pass," the fat rat whined.

The tin soldier didn't speak or move, but firmly gripped his gun in case trouble should arise. As the boat moved on, the rat ran right alongside on the tunnel ledge, huffing furiously and trembling as he gave chase.

"You haven't a pass . . . you haven't a pass?" the rat asked. "No, of course you don't! Stop then! Stop! You must pay the toll if you don't have a pass, yesss . . . yesss . . . you must pay the toll! Oh, bother! Stop him, stop him!" As he flopped his fat belly along the ledge he shouted, actually beginning to squeal commands to the sticks and bits of straw strewn along the tunnel. "He hasn't paid the toll, nooo . . . nooo . . . he hasn't paid the toll! Attention! Stop the rude fellow, you must, yesss, you must! Oh, come back here youuu . . . scoundrel! OHHHoooo, COMMMMME BAAAAACK!!!!" And as the last echoes rang along the tunnel walls the thoroughly exhausted rat fell in a heap along the ledge to have himself a good long cry.

The boat began to move faster and faster as the current gained speed. The water swirled around the tunnel and splashed up in the brave soldier's face. He could see daylight just up ahead. The end of the tunnel was near, but he felt that a greater terror was about to begin. A monstrous roar filled the air, enough to strike fear in the bravest of hearts. Oh no! The drain emptied straight into the canal! The boat would be sent tumbling down into the torrent as if it were flying off a great waterfall!

There was no time to abandon ship, this the tin soldier knew, so he held himself firm and prepared for the worst. He would have no one say of him that he flinched in the face of danger—no indeed.

The boat flew out of the drain and crashed in the water below. It whirled about at a dizzying speed; then, little by little, it began to fill with water. The little paper boat was giving way under the flood, sinking further and further into the murky deep, until the poor tin soldier found himself neck high in water. There was just time for one last look at the world around him before the water rose over his head. The paper boat gave way, and he began to sink to the bottom.

He wanted his last thoughts to be of the pretty little dancer, and he saw her twirling and whirling before him, dancing across the water with such grace and beauty! The dream brought to his ears a verse that rang deep and strong:

"Forward! Forward! Brave soldier!
From death you cannot run.
Onward! Onward! Grave warrior!
Stop not till duty's done.

"And if you should fall, do not weep,
For honor's blessing now you keep,
And none but good shall you once reap,
When life's last light doth softly retreat."

But this brave fellow's adventures did not end here, for just when it seemed that things couldn't get any worse, a large fish happened by and saw the little soldier sinking in the depths.

"Ahhh . . . what do we have here? A tasty treat, a meaty morsel, a delectable dish, a savory slice, a tantalizing tidbit, perhaps, hmmmmmmm . . . just for moi?" the fish said to himself.

Now this fine fish hailed from France, and, like many from that noble land, was quite particular about what graced his palate. He rose up from the bottom and sucked the little soldier up, swallowing him whole! And if it be known, the fish sorely regretted his action, finding the taste of toy men not at all to his liking. Well, the fish regarded his aching belly as a price one must pay in the never ending quest for finer cuisine.

The tin soldier, too, was most uncomfortable, being that it was so dark and cramped inside the fish's belly, but nevertheless he was undaunted by this state of affairs, and gripped his gun tighter, waiting for his chance to escape.

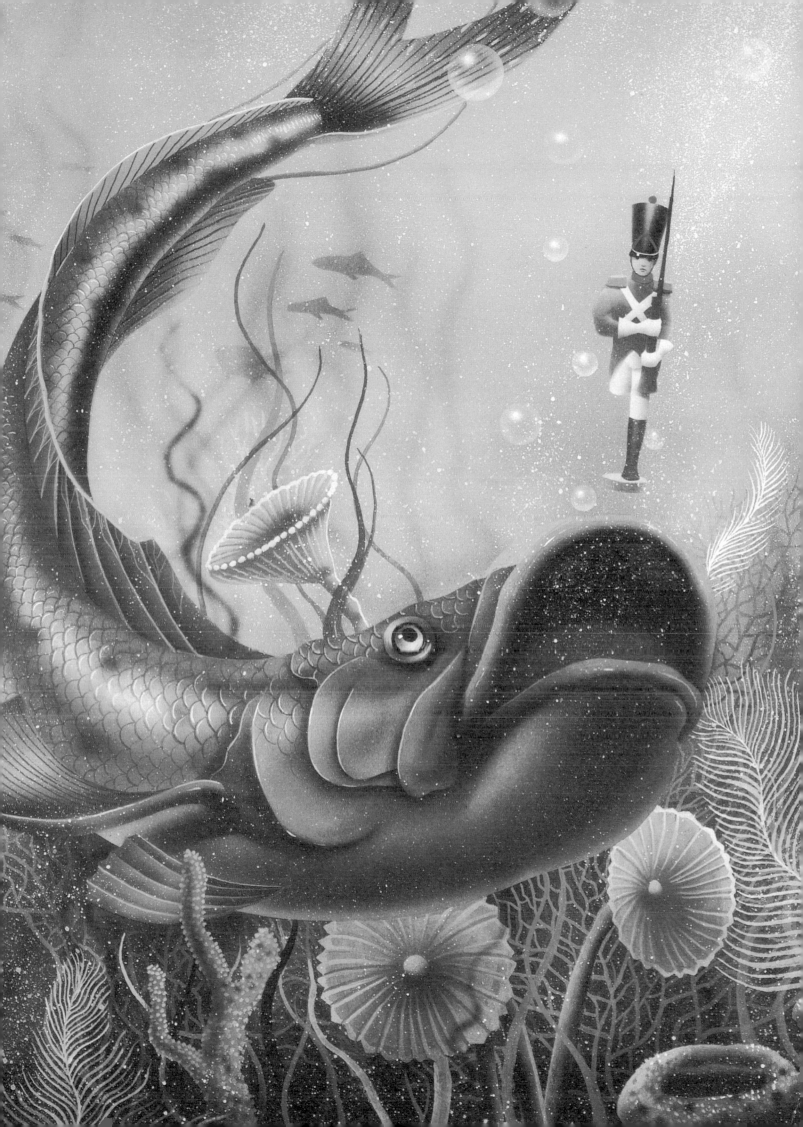

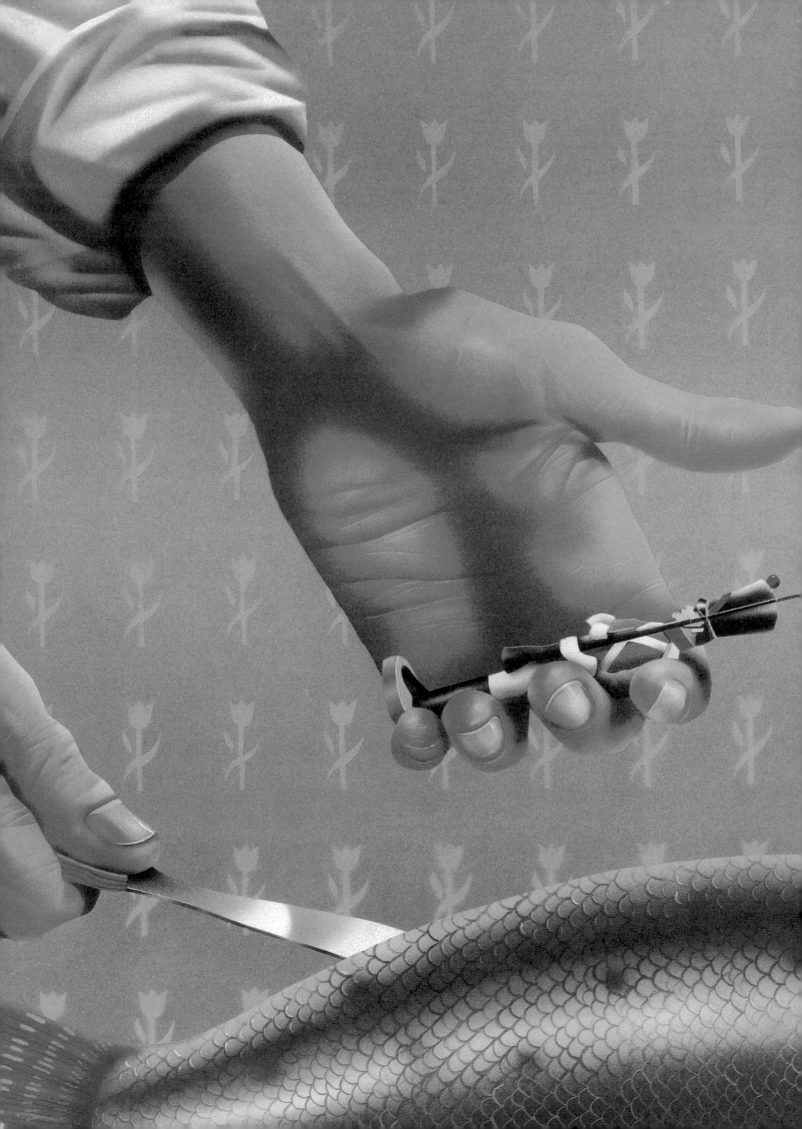

For some time he could feel the movements of the fish as it swam in the open waters, until one day the fish began to make violent jerks to and fro, then suddenly it became quite still. The next thing he knew a blinding light struck him, and a hand reached deep into the fish's belly and pulled him out to once again enjoy the sweet light of day.

"Well, by my word! A tin soldier!" a cook cried, quite amazed by her find.

You see, the fish in his search for fine food had bit just once too often and was now to be the dinner rather than the diner. He had been taken to market, sold, and was being prepared on the cutting board when the cook made her discovery.

The cook took the tin soldier into the parlor to show everyone the marvelous little man that had traveled in the belly of a fish. The tin soldier became very embarrassed, for he did not wish the world to know he had been held captive, and in such a ridiculous fashion! But wait. He knew this place! He now saw that these were the very same children, the very same toys, that he had left when he fell out of the window! And joy! There before him was the beautiful castle with the pretty little dancer, still standing on her one leg with her arms outstretched.

Ah! She too was unwavering in her life. Brave dancer! He was moved beyond words and ready to unleash a flood of joyful tears, but knew it would not be a fitting display for a soldier at arms. He looked at her and she at him, for what surely seemed like an eternity, and though they never spoke a word, they knew . . . they knew. But the world is full of goblin mischief and those who simply don't understand. At that moment one of the boys grabbed the tin soldier, and, for no reason at all, tossed him into the fireplace.

The soldier blazed up in a beautiful flame, and whether he burned from the terrific heat of the fire, or from the warm love he felt for the dancer, he simply did not know or care. He saw that all the wonderful colors of his uniform had now faded away. Had they gone because of his long and dangerous journey or had they been wiped away by his grief? He couldn't say.

He looked again at the little dancer and she looked at him. He felt his world melting away before him, but he tried his best to stand up straight and shoulder his gun as proudly as ever.

The door suddenly flew open and a gust of wind ran through the room. There he saw the little dancer begin to move. Oh! She was twirling on her one leg, high up on her tip toe. Twirling and twirling and twirling! Never had there been such a dance! Such beauty . . . such joy! Dance! Oh, Dance!

The wind moaned softly and then caught up the little dancer and carried her fluttering across the room, fluttering straight into the fire, fluttering gently to the soldier's side. She went up in flame at once, and was gone! The tin soldier was by this time melted away into a small tin lump.

When morning came and the maid started to clean away the ashes in the fireplace, she found a very strange thing indeed. At the bottom of the fireplace she found the soldier melted into the shape of a small tin heart, and deep inside the little heart, where no one would ever see, was the beautiful little spangle that the dancer had worn when she danced her glorious dance.

Copyright © 1990 Spiderwebart Inc.
Artwork © 1990 David Delamare

This edition published by Barnes & Noble, Inc.,
by arrangement with Spiderwebart Inc.

1999 Barnes & Noble Books

ISBN 0-7607-1093-7

Book design by Jennifer Ann Daddio

Printed and bound in China

99 00 01 02 03 MC 9 8 7 6 5 4 3 2 I

LFA

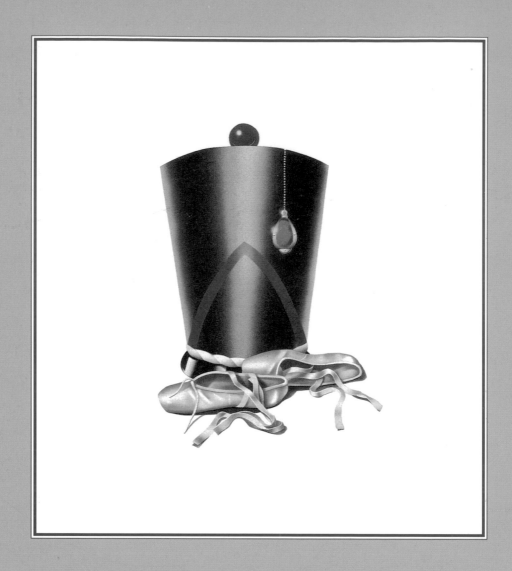